I LOVE TO KEEP MY ROOM CLEAN

Written by Shelley Admont
Illustrated by Sonal Goyal, Sumit Sakhuja

Library and Archives Canada Cataloguing in Publication data

I love to keep my room clean / Shelley Admont

ISBN: 978-1-92643207-6 paperback
ISBN: 978-1-92643208-3 hardcover
ISBN: 978-1-92643209-0 eBook

Although the author and the publisher have made every effort to ensure the
accuracy and completeness of information contained in this book, we
assume no responsibility for errors , inaccuracies, omission or any
inconsistency herein.

for those I love
the most

It was a sunny Saturday morning in a faraway forest. Three bunny brothers had just woken up.

"Good morning, boys," Mom said. "I heard you moving around in here."

"Mom, today is Saturday, we can sleep as late as we want," said the oldest brother with a smile.

"Actually, I'm still sleeping!" said the youngest brother, Jimmy.

He lay back down in his bed and closed his eyes. All of the bunny brothers and their mom started to laugh loudly.

"You can stay in your beds for a while," Mom said, "but I'll have to leave."

"I need to visit your Granny today. You'll stay with Daddy until I come back."

"When you get out of your beds and brush your teeth, you'll have your breakfast," Mom added.

"I also prepared a surprise for dessert!" All three brothers smiled, winking at each other.

"After that, you can read books or play with your toys," Mom continued. "Or, you can go outside and ride your bicycles."

"Hooray!" The bunny brothers started to jump on their beds happily.

"But..." continued Mom, "you are responsible for cleaning your room."

"Sure, Mom," answered the oldest brother proudly. "We are big enough and we can be responsible."

After they brushed their teeth, Dad served a delicious breakfast and an even more delicious dessert.

Then the fun began!

The bunnies started by putting together their puzzle. Then they continued to their wooden building blocks.

Next they played together with the rail trail before turning on the train.

"This railway train is my favorite," said Jimmy as he flipped the on switch.

The train shook the track as it moved. "This is the best present I've got on my last birthday."

After playing inside
for hours, the bunnies
grew bored.

"Let's go play outside!" said the middle brother, looking out the window.

"Yeah! But we need to clean up here first," said the older brother.

"Oh, we have enough time before Mom comes back," answered Jimmy, "we can clean up later."

The older brothers agreed and they all went out.

Outside, three bunny brothers enjoyed the sunny weather. They rode their bicycles, played hide and seek, and Simon Says.

Finally they decided to play basketball. "I don't remember where we put our basketball," said the oldest brother.

"It should be in that box with all the other sports toys," answered the middle brother.

"I think it's under my bed," added Jimmy. "Anyway, it should be somewhere in our room. I'll go check." With that, he ran inside the house, hoping to find the ball.

When he opened the door to their room he was very surprised.

The floor was covered with puzzle pieces, building blocks, cars and other toys.

Who made all this mess? thought Jimmy, making his way toward his bed.

Eventually, he stumbled and lost his balance.

He was trying to stay upright, but instead fell directly on his favorite train.

"Ouch!" he screamed, watching the train's wheels flying in different directions.

"Noooo, my favorite train!" Jimmy burst into tears.

"Are you alright, honey?" Dad appeared in the door. He couldn't fit inside the room due to all the mess.

"I'm OK. But my train..." cried Jimmy, pointing to the train's broken wheels.

"I can't even see the train," said Dad. "And what exactly happened in this room?"

"We just played...and then I fell down," Jimmy answered, tears running down his face.

"Jimmy, why's it taking you so long?" asked the other brothers as they ran into the house.

"Uh oh," said the oldest brother standing near their Dad and staring at their room.

"Did we do that?" asked the middle brother, astonished.

"My train broke!" Jimmy couldn't stop crying.

"Don't cry, Jimmy," said the oldest brother. "We'll think of something. Dad?"

"I'll check if I can fix it," answered Dad. "But you need to clean up in here."

"Bring me the train and the wheels after you find them," he said leaving the room.

"We need to hurry, before Mom comes back," said the oldest brother. He started putting the toys away and helped Jimmy get up.

"Oh, cleaning up is boring," said Jimmy sighing.

"Let's play a cleaning-up game then," exclaimed his older brother.

Jimmy became excited. "The storm is coming soon!" he shouted. "We need to help all the toys get back to their houses."

"We're superheroes," yelled the middle brother.

He picked up toys from the floor and put each one in its proper place. "We're here to help!"

They cleared everything off their beds and each one made his own bed.

Playing and enjoying, the brothers organized and cleaned everything.

"All wheels are here," exclaimed Jimmy, running to his father with the broken train in his hands.

"Here, I found the basketball!" screamed the middle brother with excitement.

"Put it in its box and...we are finished," said the oldest brother happily.

"It was really fun," said the middle brother, sitting down on his bed, "but it took us a whole hour. It was too much mess."

"No!" yelled Jimmy as he entered the room. "Don't sit there!"

"What? Why?!" asked the middle brother, jumping off the bed.

"You just made your bed. If you sit on it now, you'd have to make it again," explained Jimmy.

"Yes, I guess you're right," agreed the middle brother who remained standing near his bed.

"Maybe we could read a book now," suggested the older brother, approaching the bookshelf.

"Don't touch those books," shouted Jimmy. "I organized them all by color!"

"Sorry," said the oldest brother. "But what will we do? We can't play with anything."

Silence fell in the room. They thought for a while and then the oldest brother shouted: "I have an idea!"

The two younger brothers listened to him very carefully.

"We can clean up after each game," he suggested. "Then it won't take so much time."

"Let's try," said Jimmy happily.

First, the oldest brother read a beautiful book with pop-up pictures to his brothers. When they finished reading, he put it back on the shelf.

Next, they built a large tower out of their colorful blocks. When they were done, they put the blocks back into the box — and the room stayed clean!

At that moment, Mom and Dad knocked on the door. The brothers ran to hug their Mom.

"I missed you so much," said Mom, "but I see you managed to keep your room clean. I'm so proud of you."

"And here's your train, Jimmy," said Dad, handing him the toy. The wheels were fixed and Jimmy smiled widely.

"Who wants to try cookies that Granny made for you?" asked Mom.

"Me!" shouted the bunny brothers and their Dad.

"But we'll eat them in the kitchen, not in this clean room," said Jimmy very seriously. "Right, Mom?"

The whole family started laughing loudly and went to the kitchen to eat cookies.

Since that day, the brothers loved to keep their room clean and organized.

They played with all their toys but when they finished, they put everything back in its place.

It never took them long to clean up their room again.

MORE GREAT BOOKS BY SHELLEY ADMONT
Collect them all!

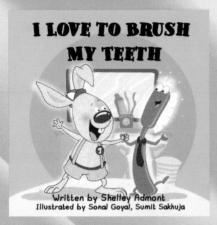

I LOVE TO BRUSH MY TEETH
Written by Shelley Admont
Illustrated by Sonal Goyal, Sumit Sakhuja

I LOVE MY MOM
Written by Shelley Admont
Illustrated by Sonal Goyal, Sumit Sakhuja

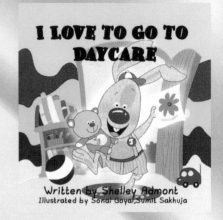

I LOVE TO GO TO DAYCARE
Written by Shelley Admont
Illustrated by Sonal Goyal, Sumit Sakhuja

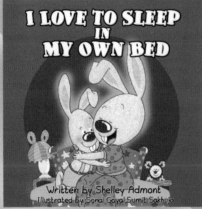

I LOVE TO SLEEP IN MY OWN BED
Written by Shelley Admont
Illustrated by Sonal Goyal, Sumit Sakhuja

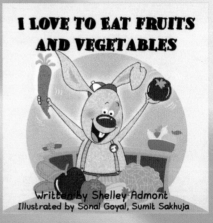

I LOVE TO EAT FRUITS AND VEGETABLES
Written by Shelley Admont
Illustrated by Sonal Goyal, Sumit Sakhuja

Written by Shelley Admont
AMANDA'S DREAM
Illustrated by Sumana Roy

Written by Shelley Admont
AMANDA and the LOST TIME
Illustrated by Humpty Dumpty

56034613R00023

Made in the USA
Lexington, KY
10 October 2016